Pumpkin Soup

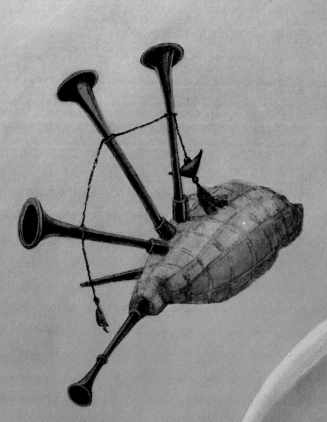

A PICTURE CORGI BOOK: 0 552 545104

First published in Great Britain by Doubleday, a division of
Random House Children's Books

PRINTING HISTORY
Doubleday edition published 1998
Picture Corgi edition published 1999

13 15 17 19 20 18 16 14 12

Picture Corgi Books are published by Random House Children's Books
61-63 Uxbridge Road, London W5 5SA,
a division of The Random House Group Ltd,
in Australia by Random House Australia (Pty) Ltd,
20 Alfred Street, Milsons Point, Sydney, NSW 2061, Australia,
in New Zealand by Random House New Zealand Ltd,
18 Poland Road, Glenfield, Auckland 10, New Zealand
and in South Africa by Random House (Pty) Ltd,
Endulini, 5a Jubilee Road, Parktown 2193, South Africa

Printed in Singapore
www.wormworks.com

To
Jomai
and
Max

PumPKin SouP

Helen Cooper

Picture Corgi Books

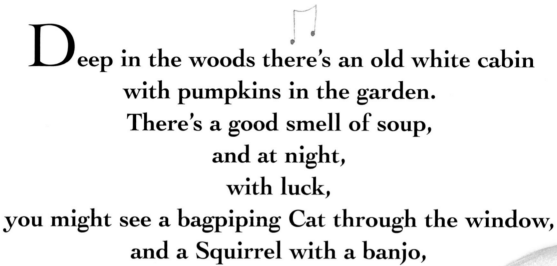

Deep in the woods there's an old white cabin
with pumpkins in the garden.
There's a good smell of soup,
and at night,
with luck,
you might see a bagpiping Cat through the window,
and a Squirrel with a banjo,
and a small singing Duck.

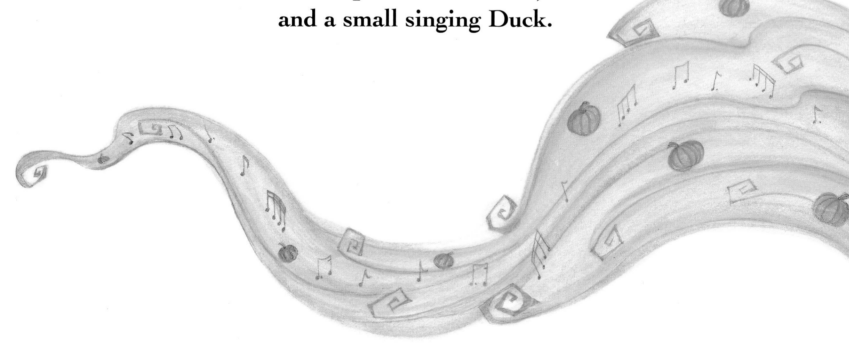

Pumpkin Soup.
The best you ever tasted.

Made by the Cat who slices up the pumpkin.

Made by the Squirrel who stirs in the water.

Made by the Duck who scoops up a pipkin of salt, and tips in just enough.

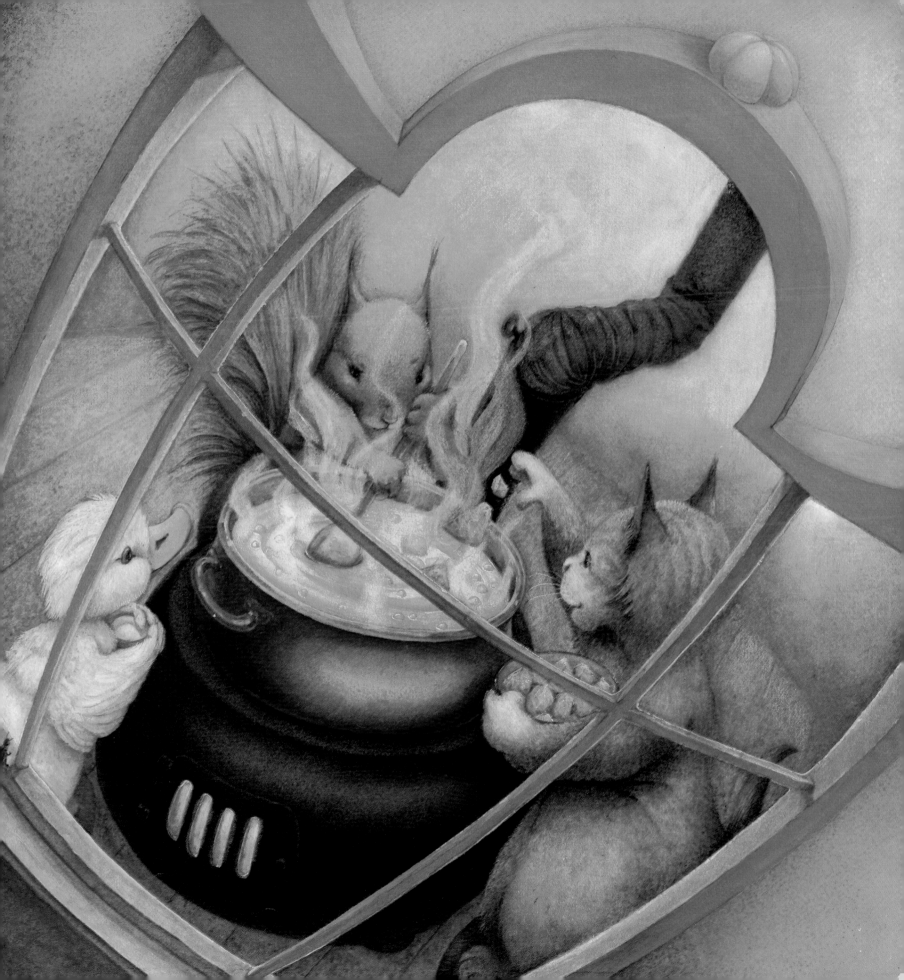

They slurp their soup,

and play their song,

then pop off to bed,
in a quilt stitched together by the Cat,
embroidered by the Squirrel
and filled with fine feathers from the Duck.

And it's peaceful in the old white cabin.
Everyone has his own job to do.
Everyone is happy.
Or so it seems . . .

But one morning the Duck
woke up early.
He tiptoed into the kitchen
and smiled at the
Squirrel's special spoon.
"Wouldn't it be fine," he murmured,
"if I could be the Head Cook."

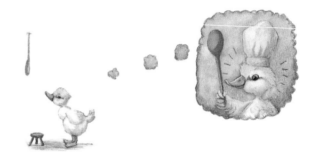

He drew up a stool,
hopped on top
and reached . . .
until his beak just touched
the tip of the spoon . . .

KER-PLONK!

Down it clattered.

Then the Duck trotted
back to the bedroom,
held up the spoon
and said,
"Today it's *my* turn to stir the soup."

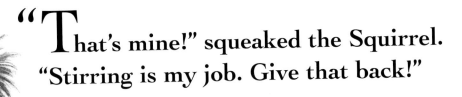

"That's mine!" squeaked the Squirrel.
"Stirring is my job. Give that back!"

"You're much too small," snapped the Cat.
"We'll cook the way we always have."

But the Duck held on tight . . .
. . . until the Squirrel tugged with all his might . . .
. . . and – WHOOPS! –
the spoon spun through the air,
and bopped the Cat on the head.

Then there was trouble,
a horrible squabble,
a row,
a racket,
a rumpus
in the old white cabin.

TOK!

"I'm not staying here," wailed the Duck.
"You never let me help with anything."
And he packed up a barrow,
put on his hat
and waddled away.

"You'll be back," stormed the Cat,
"after we've cleaned up."
And the Squirrel shook his spoon in the air.
But the Duck didn't come back.

Not for breakfast.

Not even for lunch.

"I'll find him," scoffed the Cat.
"He'll be hiding outside."

"I bet he's in the pumpkin patch."

But the Duck was not in the pumpkin patch.
They could not find him anywhere.

So they waited.
All that long afternoon.

The Cat watched the door,

the Squirrel paced the floor.

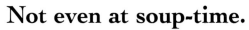

"That Duck will be sorry when he comes home," they muttered.
But the Duck didn't come home.
Not even at soup-time.

The soup wasn't tasty.
They'd made it too salty.
They didn't feel hungry anyway.
They both sobbed over supper,
and their tears dripped into the soup
and made it even saltier.

"We should have let him stir the soup,"
sniffed the Squirrel.
"He was only trying to help," wept the Cat.
"Let's go out and look for him."

The Cat and the Squirrel were scared
as they wandered down the path,
in the dark dark woods.

They feared for the Duck all alone with the trees,
and the foxes,
and the wolves,
and the witches,
and the bears.

But they couldn't find him.

On and on
they trotted.
They reached the edge
of a steep steep cliff.

"Maybe he fell down that!"
wailed the Cat.

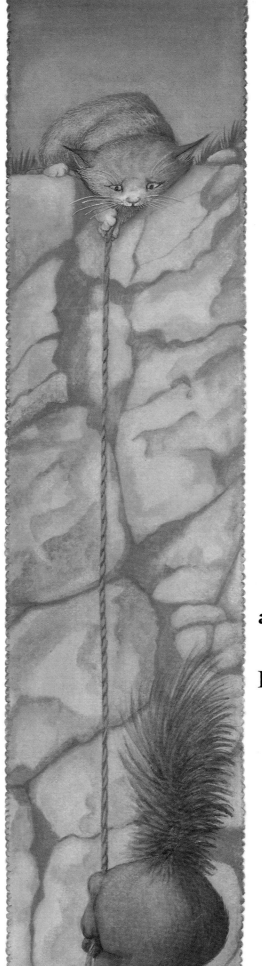

"I'll save him,"
squeaked the Squirrel,
and he scrambled down
on a long shaky rope.
He searched all around,
on the ground.
But he couldn't
find the Duck.

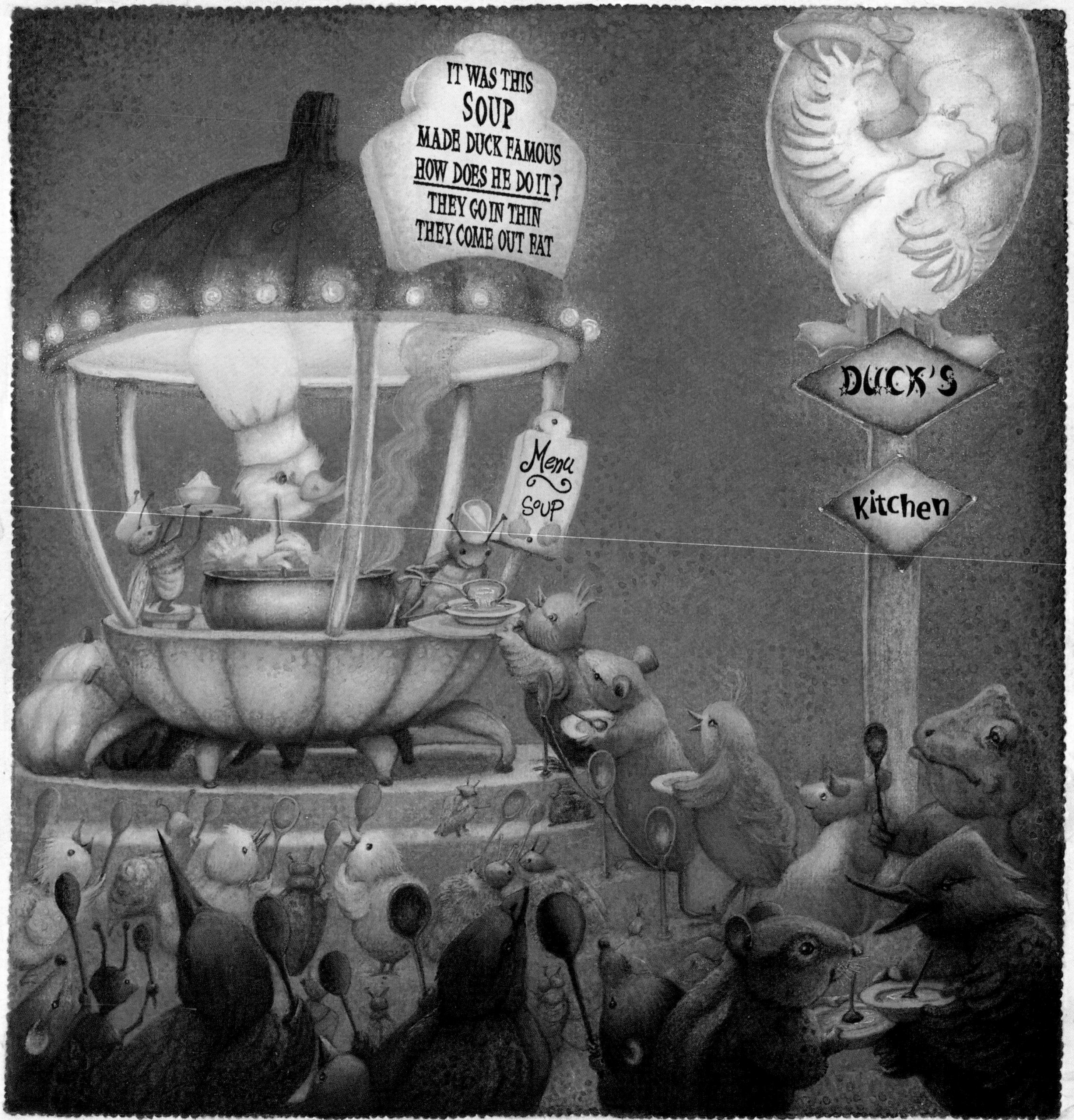

IT WAS THIS
SOUP
MADE DUCK FAMOUS
HOW DOES HE DO IT?
THEY GO IN THIN
THEY COME OUT FAT

Menu
SOUP

DUCK'S

Kitchen

Then the Cat whispered in a sad little voice,
"Duck might have found some better friends."
"He might," yelped the Squirrel.
"Friends who let him help."

And the more they thought about it,
as they plodded back,
the more they were sure they were right.

But when they were almost home,
they saw light shining
from the old white cabin.

"It's Duck!" they shrieked,
as they burst through the door.

And Duck was *so* pleased to see them.

He was also very hungry,
and though it was late,
they thought they would all make . . .

...Some
Pumpkin
Soup.

W hen the Duck stirred, the Cat and the Squirrel didn't say a word.

Not even when the Duck stirred the soup so fast
that it slopped right out of the pot.

Not even when the pot got burnt.

Then the Duck showed the Squirrel how to measure out the salt.
And the soup was still the best you ever tasted.

So once again it was peaceful
in the old white cabin.

Until the Duck said...

..."I think I'll play the bagpipes now."